Mermaid & Monster
Stories from the Sea

Other Mammoth story collections

Scary Stories   edited by Valerie Bierman
Snake on the Bus   edited by Valerie Bierman
Prima Ballerina   edited by Miriam Hodgson

Also by Grace Hallworth

Cric Crac
Down by the River
(Highly Commended for the Kate Greenaway Medal)
A Web of Stories

Mermaid & Monster

Stories from the Sea

GRACE HALLWORTH

Illustrated by Bernard Lodge

Mammoth

In Memory of Marcus Crouch who was an inspiration

First published in Great Britain in 1997
by Mammoth
an imprint of Reed International Books Ltd
Michelin House, 81 Fulham Road, London SW3 6RB
and Auckland and Melbourne

ISBN 0 7497 2858 2

10 9 8 7 6 5 4 3 2 1

A CIP catalogue record for this title
is available from the British Library

Typeset by Avon Dataset Ltd, Bidford on Avon, B50 4JH
Printed in Great Britain by Cox & Wyman Ltd, Reading,
Berkshire

Contents

Part Two:
Sea Monsters

About the Stories

Since I began collecting stories about water creatures, I have discovered a number of people who are equally fascinated by them, whether as flesh and blood creatures, or as imaginative creations. This collection is, therefore, in the nature of a collaborative effort and includes stories which were shared in a variety of contexts.

I am grateful to Professor Dov Noy, Chair of Folklore at the Hebrew University of Jerusalem, who provided me with background information about Atargatis, the first recorded mermaid. Hers is a story waiting to be told in the real sense.

I am also indebted to Hartley Neita of Jamaica, who generously gave permission to retell and include the legend *The Mermaid's Comb* retold in *Anansesem: a collection of Caribbean folk tales, legends and poems for juniors* (pub. Longman Jamaica Ltd., 1985). I have retold it under the title *The Mermaid's Rock*.

During a workshop in Dublin, fourteen-year-old Aoife Kelly recounted a legend about the transformation of a seal into a woman. I have developed her story in *The Seal Woman*. It was also at a storytelling festival in Dublin that I was told the story of *The Lonely Fisherman* by Scottish storyteller, David Campbell. He had been told it by George McPherson of Glendale, Isle of Skye. I have been moved to retell that story in my own way.

I hope that you will enjoy the stories in this collection and will find your own voice in retelling them.

Grace Hallworth

August 1997

In the Beginning

Many people believe that all life began in the sea. The Babylonians worshipped Oannes, the great fish of the ocean, as the supreme god. He was a being, both fish and human. Under the fish's head was the head of a man, and under the fish's tail, feet like a man's were joined. Like the sun he rose from the waves every morning and disappeared at night into the sea.[1]

In the Ute and Pueblo traditions, mermen are said to be the original beings from outer space, Kua-ouu-teh. They also lived in the ocean by night. During the day these enlightened beings instructed the people in arts and sciences, and taught them respect for life.[2]

[1] Beatrice Phillpots *Mermaids* NY Ballantine Books 1980
[2] Joseph E. Rael *Beautiful Painted Arrow: stones and teachings from Native American Tradition* Element 1992

1

According to Babylonian legends, those who dwelt in the divine waters, or descended into them, were honoured as gods and goddesses. One of these legends tells about Atargatis, a beautiful woman who, as a result of an unhappy love affair, plunged into a sacred pool and emerged as a fish. She was later deified as a goddess of fertility and portrayed as a mermaid, the first in recorded history. The upper part of her body was said to be that of a woman but from the thigh downwards, was in the form of a fish.

Water appears to be an essential element for many of the beings and spirits which influence the lives of human beings. Some Indian tribes of South America believe that the guardian of the river is a water mama, whom the Arawaks call Oriyu. The River Muma of Jamaican legend may have travelled from Africa, where there is a belief that rivers have a spirit guardian. But her appearance as a woman with long, jet-black hair resembles the water mama of the Arawaks.

Water beings are often attracted to humans and will try to lure them to their homes in the deep. Sometimes these beings will agree to live on land with their human partner, who must abide by certain conditions. Selkies are seals in the sea but become beautiful women – and handsome men – when they come ashore and cast off their skins. Their beauty makes them desirable to men who may chance on them, seize their skins and force them to become partners and wives. Until the woman finds her skin she is unable to return to the sea. A similar fate visits the Welsh mermaid whose fish-skin cap enables her to pass through the water. If that is taken away when she is on land, she is compelled to remain there.

When living creatures were emerging, there appeared also monstrous beasts, and leviathans which inhabit sea, river and lake. Leviathan of the Bible may owe its existence in sea lore to the Canaanite myth about Lotan, a seven-headed serpent which was destroyed by Baal. Serpents and dragons that live in water form part of the cultural traditions of many different groups. The Indians of the Amazon consider the Mai d'agoa, a pythonesque snake, to be the guardian of the Wild Lake of the Amazon. And in Trinidad, Mama de l'eau is the being who guards the rivers. From the waist upwards she has the body of a woman with long, fair hair or black hair. But the lower part of her body is in the form of a houilla, a serpent with a razor-sharp, whip-like tail.

Sedna, the Eskimo goddess, realised her power when she was thrown into the sea. The Inuit (the human beings) believe that the animals of the sea are her creatures formed from drops of her blood and from her fingers which were chopped off by her father when she clung to his kayak.

Part One

Mermaids, Mermen and Selkies

Grethe and the Merman
Denmark

In a seaside village in Denmark, there lived a couple who had an only child. Her given name was Margaret but she was called Grethe by everyone who knew her. The girl loved her parents very much and it grieved her to see how hard they worked to put one meagre meal on the table every day. So, when Grethe was no longer a child, she used to take her basket and go down to the sea to collect whatever she could find to sell in the market.

One morning Grethe was up to her knees in water gathering mussels and small fishes when a merman appeared. Before the girl could flee, he called, 'Grethe, do not be afraid. If you are brave enough to come with me, you will find enough gold and silver coins to make you rich for the rest of your life.'

The merman was pleasing to look at and his manner was friendly. Grethe thought of her parents who were getting on in years. A handful of silver coins would certainly provide comfort for their old age. She agreed to go with him.

Down she went, her hand held fast by the merman, who dived swiftly to the bottom of the sea. There she saw a room stacked high with gold and silver coins, and other rooms filled with the most beautiful treasures. But when Grethe asked for a sack in which to put some coins, the merman laughed.

'Did you believe I would give you gold and silver for nothing?' he sneered.

'What do you want from me?' Grethe asked.

'Stay here with me for seven years and you may have as many coins as you wish.'

Grethe was greatly troubled. She was certain that the merman would never allow her to return to her home. How would she know when seven years had passed in the timeless world in the depths of the sea? But Grethe was a sensible girl. She displayed neither the anger nor the panic she was feeling. She pretended to agree and told the merman, 'I will stay with you for seven years and not a moment more.'

However she intended to find a way to escape at the first opportunity.

The days lengthened into weeks and the weeks stretched into months. Before she knew it, Grethe had been with the merman for three years, and was the mother of three children. In all that time, although she kept her eyes and ears open, she found no way to escape her prison under the sea.

One day the sea was unusually calm. The air was quite still and the sun cast a reddish glow over the water. Drifting through it was the sound of church bells ringing, calling the people to worship. Grethe had not heard that sound since she had left the land, and it brought back memories of her parents. If they were alive they would be attending the service at the little church, which stood on a grassy knoll not far from the sea. The three of them used to worship there every Sunday without fail, and Grethe loved nothing better than singing the hymns and chanting the psalms.

Tears filled her eyes and ran down her cheeks as the memories came flooding in. The merman had never seen her in such a state and was confused. Until now pride would not let her reveal her sadness to him, a creature she despised because he had deceived her.

'Grethe, what ails you that you weep so?' he asked.

'Oh, my poor parents! Two old people with no one to help them. How they must be suffering from cold and hunger! And I, their only child in a place filled with gold and silver.' And she sobbed even louder.

The merman couldn't bear to see her weeping. Besides

he didn't want the children to witness her grief. He said to her, 'Come now, dry your tears, Grethe. I will arrange for you to visit your parents. I know they are still alive. Take them enough gold and silver coins to provide all their needs.'

The girl hurried to the room where the coins were stored and filled as many sacks as she could carry. Then, kissing her three children, she followed the merman through a cave that led to the beach. The church was within calling distance.

'I'll wait here for you, Grethe. Do not linger. Remember the children are waiting.' Grethe promised to return quickly.

The pastor was preaching the sermon when Grethe crept into the church and took a seat at the back. His words were like a draught of cool water on a parched throat.

In the middle of the sermon she heard the merman calling, 'Grethe! Grethe! Remember your children are waiting.'

She heard him plainly enough but resolved within herself to hear the sermon out. Some of the congregation, who had heard the voice, looked around to see who was causing the disturbance. But they saw no one and turned their attention back to the pastor.

Soon the sermon ended and the closing hymn was announced. Before the singing could begin, the merman called a second time, 'Grethe! Grethe! Come away now. Remember your children are waiting.'

Now, more members of the congregation were looking around to see who was calling. The organist had begun to play the final hymn. Grethe was determined not to leave before she had joined in the singing.

Her parents had heard their daughter's pet name, and turned around to see who was calling her. They spotted Grethe at the back of the church and ran to embrace her. Just then the merman again called, 'Grethe! Grethe! Your children need you.' Her parents held her close. They did not want her to leave. The pastor went to the door and saw the merman at the edge of the water.

At the back of the church there was a font of holy water used for christenings. The pastor took the font from its pedestal and sprinkled the holy water as he walked to the beach, crying in a loud voice, 'Begone, unholy creature. Depart to the world for which you were created and to which you belong. Torment no more the mortals of this world!'

A heartrending cry came from the merman, who dived to the bottom of the sea and was never seen above the water again. Grethe knew she had to leave the children and stay with her parents. She looked after them for as long as they lived.

People of that village say that, on a clear day, when the

sea is calm and the air is still, if you are near the sea you can hear the merman calling from the depths of the sea, 'Grethe! Grethe! Will you not return to me? I am waiting, waiting. Waiting . . .'

The Seal Woman
Ireland

A farmer used to go down to the seashore for seaweed to spread over his field. One day, as he came to the beach, he saw a woman trying to staunch the flow of blood from her feet. But no matter how much she washed them the bleeding would not stop.

The farmer had never seen the woman before, but when she looked at him with her green eyes so full of pain he was moved to help her.

'You'll not be walking on those feet for many a day. Come rest at my cottage until they are healed.' He did not wait for an answer but wrapped his shirt around her naked body and carried her up the path to his farmhouse.

Later that day, when he returned to the beach, he saw the skin of a seal between some rocks. He was certain it belonged to the woman and at first, thought to take it to her. Then he thought again and threw the skin into the sea.

By the time the woman was able to walk again the farmer had grown accustomed to her company. She did her share of work in the house and on the farm but there was no love between them. She was bonded to her three seal children left behind in the sea.

One night, when the farmer was asleep, she went down to the sea and searched the beach for her sealskin, but could not find it. When she told the farmer she would stay with him he said nothing. Secretly he was pleased, for he had been lonely since his wife died.

Some time later the seal woman gave birth to a child. A strange boy with sea-green eyes and webbed fingers and toes, who never smiled and never cried. And although she often went down to the water, searching the sea as far as the eye could scan, she kept her child from the sea.

Almost nine months after the child was born there was a terrible storm. The waves dashed themselves against the shore as though the sea were in a rage, and the night was filled with moaning sounds like the cries of creatures in great pain.

'Did you ever hear the like of that?' said the farmer. ''Tis as mournful a cry as the banshee call!'

The woman said not a word.

Each night the wailing sounds grew louder, came ever closer, until on the third night they were right outside the farmhouse.

14

The child began to cry for the first time since he was born. It was a cry of fear and anger.

'Whatever is disturbing our nights now comes to frighten the child. I will put a stop to it once and for all,' said the farmer angrily.

'No, let me attend to it,' said the woman.

She rose from her bed and went to the door and cried, 'Cease your wailing and leave us be.'

The noise grew louder. So the woman stepped outside. At once there was silence.

After a while, when the woman did not return to bed, the farmer went to see what was keeping her. There was no one outside the house nor down to the beach. The storm had blown itself out and, in the light of the moon, the farmer saw a broad swath of damp earth leading from the house to the water. Tufts of grey fur were caught on the rough edges of the gate posts. There was no sign of the woman. Her seal children had taken her back to the sea.

All night long the farmer was kept awake by the crying of his son. He rocked the babe and tried to croon to him the way his mother did, but the child would not be comforted.

'The seals have robbed you of a mother's warmth and a mother's milk,' he said bitterly.

Early next morning he heard a commotion outside, and looking out, saw a large white cow standing in the middle of the field, surrounded by the farmer's brown cows. Astounded, he went outside to examine the animal, for he had never seen a white cow before. It was a magnificent creature with soft brown eyes and udders weighted down with milk. Whenever it shook itself, jets of water were sprayed in every direction. Some fell on the farmer's face and tasted salty like sea water. He filled a pitcher of creamy fresh milk from the cow and gave it to the child, who stopped crying as soon as he tasted the milk.

From that moment he would take milk from none other but the white cow.

The boy grew healthy and strong and worked hard on his father's farm, but he was a lonely lad with no friends. The people had distrusted his mother and they did not accept her son.

'It's not natural!' they said. 'He never laughs like other children but looks past you with those strange green eyes. Just like his mother!'

The boy knew nothing about his mother, except what his father told him. It was the same story he told everyone who asked about her: that she went walking on the beach one stormy night and was swept into the sea. And yet the boy loved the sea. He often went swimming among the seals, who came to the island to sun themselves on the rocks. And they had no fear of him.

As soon as he was old enough, the lad joined a fishing

fleet, which fished the deep waters for sharks, swordfish, whales and other large fish. He refused to work with anyone who hunted his friends, the seals.

When he told his father how much he loved the sea, his father said, 'You are all the kin I have and the farm will be yours when I am dead. Will you turn away from your inheritance?'

The son replied, 'I know I should stay and help you on the farm, but the sea calls and I must go.'

When the father heard this he was troubled. He feared that the boy's seal mother was drawing him to her in the sea. Still, he did not reveal the truth about the seal woman to his son, but bade him Godspeed, believing he would never see him again.

At the end of a week's fishing the fleet was returning home when a storm blew up. Many of the fishing boats were swamped and the men flung into the sea. When the farmer's son found himself in the water he saw a large seal swimming towards him. As it dived beneath him he put his arms round its neck and felt himself being carried through the water until he was set on firm ground. The seal had taken him to a small island, but the lad had no idea where he was. Exhausted from the buffeting of the waves he fell into a deep sleep.

He didn't know how long he slept, but when he awoke he saw a beautiful woman lying close to him. She was naked and there was a soft sheen over her pale, white skin. Through the strands of silky, green hair that covered her face, he could see long, black eyelashes. A black sealskin was tucked around him. As he stirred, the woman opened her eyes. They were as green as his own. In that moment he knew that she was his mother. And she, looking into his eyes knew that he had recognised her, without knowing why.

'Did your father never tell you what happened?' she asked.

'No,' said the lad. 'But why did you leave us?'

'When your father found me among the rocks, he took me to his farm and threw away my skin. My seal babes found it and came looking for me. They had no one to care for them, but you had a father who loved you.'

'Did *you* not love me?' asked the boy.

'Yes, very much, and I never deserted you. I sent you the cow whose milk fed and nurtured you. Your brothers and I played with you on the rocks, and swam with you in the sea. I followed your boat when it sailed so far away from land, and stayed close to save you when you were thrown into the sea. I kept watch over you for two days while you slept and gave you my coat to keep you warm.'

The lad was ashamed of doubting her love. He knew the dangers she risked in following the fleet into waters where there were so many fish that preyed on seals. Even there on a deserted island they could be surprised by men who might harm her. He begged her to put on her sealskin, but she would not as long as he needed it. Each day she went in search of fresh water and fished for whatever she could find close by on the beach and in the sea, until her son was strong enough to look after himself. While they were together she taught him the lore of the sea, and of those creatures which lived in the sea.

One day she said to him, 'Soon I shall leave you and return as a seal to the sea. Remember always that you are of the seal people as well as of the land people. When you are in need of them the seals will help you.'

The following morning when he awoke she was gone, but in the distance he saw a fishing boat making its way to the island. The men were surprised to see someone on the beach. They said they were lured to the island by a large shoal of fish fleeing from a black seal.

The lad was taken back to his island and his father was overjoyed to see him alive. The few fishermen who had returned from the storm had said that none of the men whose boats had been capsized, had survived. Many people in the village regarded his safe return as a miracle, but there were those who had their doubts.

'There's always been something strange about that boy and his mother!' they said. 'He never laughed even as a child, and he has webbed fingers and those green eyes that look past you. Just like his mother!'

But now that the lad knew of his connection with the sea, he no longer yearned to be there. He stayed on the farm and helped his father, but often he would go down to the sea and swim among the seals that came to sun themselves on the rocks. And somehow the community began to accept him.

After a while he married a girl from the village, and filled the farmhouse with children who laughed and cried and swam among the seals. And everyone of those children had sea-green eyes, and fingers and toes that were webbed!

The Seal Hunt
Ireland

One day three men go out to hunt seals and spot three large ones. They pursue the seals and strike at them with their clubs. Suddenly a storm arises and strong winds drive the curragh away from the seals, who quickly swim away from the men towards the land. Soon the skies become so black that the men cannot tell whether they are heading out to sea or drifting towards land.

As the storm rages, the curragh is tossed from wave crest to trough until the men lose all hope of being saved. In the distance they see a light which they hope will lead them to safety. After rowing with all the strength they can muster, they find themselves at the edge of a small island which is not known to any of them.

On the highest point of the island there is a lone cottage, with neither tree nor shrub to keep it company. The men are uneasy. There is something eerie about the place but

21

they dare not remain at sea as long as the wind blows so fiercely.

They pull their curragh on to the beach and secure it. Then they climb the hill to the cottage.

Inside the cottage three men are stretched out on the floor and an old woman is putting poultices on their backs. They are red and blue with bruising.

'What happened to your backs?' asks one of the hunters. 'Were you dashed against the rocks in the storm?'

The youngest of the hunters remains silent. An idea has just occurred to him, filling him with unease. Before he can warn the other hunters, one of the wounded men replies, 'Shouldn't you know what happened to us! 'Tis yourselves who this very day nearly clubbed us to death.'

When they hear this the hunters fear for their lives. Even if they manage to reach their boat they cannot put out to sea since the wind is blowing harder than ever.

'You are right to be angry,' says the youngest hunter, 'but before you take revenge, let me remind you that there were times when humans defended you with no thought for the safety of their lives. My grandfather, John Curley, was such a man.'

The oldest of the seal men looks at the young man keenly for a long time. 'Aye son, you speak the truth and all. He stood against a band of hunters who would have killed my young one and its mother, when they rested on the rocks one day,' says the old one. 'For the sake of your grandfather you are all free to leave this island. But first promise that you will never again hunt the seal.' Each man gives a solemn promise and suddenly the storm ends.

The Lonely Fisherman
～ *The Scottish Isles* ～

There was once a fisherman who lived in a cottage by the sea. He had lived in the same village all his life yet no man would fish with him and no woman would marry him. All because of a birthmark that blazed across his face from brow to chin.

'Auld Clootie himself set his mark on the boy. The devil claims him body and soul,' so the story went.

Lonely and friendless, the fisherman walked along the shore listening to the waves when, far out at sea, they roared as they broke over the reefs. He listened to the waves when, close to land, they whispered their secrets to the sand. In time he learned the language of the sea. She was his only friend.

One day he saw a woman sitting on a rock combing her long, golden hair. She was as naked as a newborn babe. As he drew close he saw a sealskin lying beside her and knew that she was a selkie, a seal woman. Quietly he came forward and quickly he got hold of the skin. No matter how much she begged him to return it, he would not.

'If you want the skin, come home with me for a while,' he said.

Finally she agreed to go with him to his cottage.

When he got home he thought about how lonely he was, and how much he wanted someone to love, and to be loved. He hid the sealskin where she could not find it.

That night she touched the raw, red welt on the fisherman's face.

'Who bruised your face so badly?' she asked.

'The devil set me apart from others with his sign,' the fisherman said bitterly. 'Because of this I am an outcast in my own village.'

When the woman heard this she was filled with pity for him and agreed to stay and share his life. Yet she hoped to find the sealskin and return one day to the sea.

But not in the first months, nor in the first years did she find it. As time passed her feelings for the fisherman changed to an earthly love and they became truly man and wife.

Often, as the fisherman walked along the beach, he listened to the waves murmuring to the pebbles. They seemed to say, 'Send her back to her kingdom and her kin. 'Tis not right to hold her against her will.'

One night he said to her, 'I cannot bear to part with you but I will tell you where I have hidden the sealskin so that you may return to your folk.'

But she said, 'I have no wish to leave you. Let the skin remain in its hiding place.'

And now the fisherman was happier than he had ever been in his whole life.

Soon the woman bore him three children: two boys and a girl. One day the youngest child, the daughter, was playing in the shed amongst the nets and lines, and as she rummaged she found a wooden box. Inside was a beautiful pelt of finest silver-grey fur. The child ran into the house to show her mother. Immediately the mother saw it she was filled with such a yearning to return to the sea, she could deny it no more. She heard the voices of the selkies singing, calling her back to the deep. And she was torn between an earthly love for her man and family, and for the sea that surged in her blood.

When the fisherman returned home that evening she told him what had happened, and of her deep longing to return to the sea.

'I love you still,' she said to him, 'and to lose you would be like losing another skin grown from our love of these past fifteen years. But I cannot help myself. I must answer the call.'

The fisherman was desolate at losing her, but he would

not hold her against her will. Before she left she said to him, 'If the time should come when you have need of me, and the children no longer need you, come to the place where we first met. Call me and I will answer your call.'

Then she put on the sealskin and at once was changed into a beautiful seal that slipped into the water and was gone.

One by one as the children became adults they left home until, once again, the fisherman was alone. Alone in his cottage by the sea with nothing but his memories. He went about his fishing without heart.

One day, as he wandered the shore, he remembered his wife's last promise. It was as though the little waves that lapped the shore were whispering words with her soft voice: 'If the time should come when you have need of me, and the children no longer need you, come to the place where we first met. Call me and I will answer your call.'

At once he went to the rock where he first saw her and called to her. Out of the sea came an answering cry and through the waves his seal wife came to him.

'Come now and join me in our kingdom under the sea,' she said. And reaching out to him she led him down, down into the green depths of the sea. Down to a place where everything was a shimmer of green light. Where green sea grass eddied and flowed, moved by quiet currents under the ocean. Where pearls glinted on white sand.

And they were happy and joyous together.

Timeless and tranquil was their life under the sea and they yearned for no one or nothing. Until, as if in a dream, the fisherman's wife saw the birth of a child to their daughter. For the first time since he left the land the fisherman felt an urge to return.

'I must see our first grandchild,' he said to his wife, 'even if it is to hold the bairn in my arms for a brief moment.'

'Then I will go with you,' said the wife. 'But if we return we lose our immortality and can never re-enter the kingdom under the sea. Nor can we live on land.'

'So be it,' said the fisherman.

The two set out together, and when they came to the shore they took human form. Hand in hand they walked to the old cottage by the sea, where their daughter now lived. She was overcome with joy, for she never thought to see her parents again. She took them to where the child lay in his cradle.

He was a lovely bonny boy who gurgled and laughed when his grandparents picked him up and kissed him, as though he had known them always. When they laid him back in his cradle, each placed the hanselling gift they had brought with them from the very depths of the ocean. A beautiful pearl lay on either side of the child's pillow. Then, as dusk came down, they bade their daughter a last farewell and left the cottage. Hand in hand they walked back towards the shore.

Next morning the dead bodies of a female and a male seal were found halfway between house and sea, with their flippers entwined.

The Mermaid's Rock
Jamaica

On the island of Jamaica there is a tall cliff. At the foot of the cliff there is a large pool where the women gather to wash their clothes during the day. But at night the pool is deserted, an eerie place full of mystery and foreboding. No one visits the pool at night except the foolhardy, and those who don't know the legend.

Folk say that at the edge of the pool there was once a rock, a rough, white mass of stone. On moonlit nights, it glowed with a strange, unearthly light that set the pool ablaze. They say that this rock was the throne of a mermaid called Dora, who used to sit combing her long, silky, green-tinted hair, humming softly to herself.

The tune she hummed was beautiful, yet sad and haunting too. And although the song had no words, to all who heard it, the meaning was clear. It was a promise that what they most desired would be granted to them. When

Dora heard someone approaching she would dive into the pool, leaving her comb on the rock. From under the water she would sing her wordless song, and this was her message:

> 'Take my comb
> Return to your home
> And I will come to you in your dream.
> Take my comb
> Return to your home
> And I will give you your heart's desire
> Soo-oo-oooo-oon.'

Not far away from the pool lived a girl called Hazel. Her father was a very wealthy man and Hazel had everything she desired . . . well, almost everything. Her father could not give her the one thing she most wanted. Hazel longed for hair that flowed down her back. Hair that was as soft as the finest silk. Hair that sparkled in the moonlight. She had tried everything – conditioners, creams, oils, shampoos of all kinds, even common garden herbs. All in vain. Sleeping and waking, Hazel thought of nothing but long, silky hair. She spent nearly all her inheritance travelling from one salon to another, from one city to another, from one continent to another, to find the magic treatment that would transform her hair and satisfy her longing.

Hazel knew the legend of the mermaid on the rock, but at first she didn't believe a word of it. However, after a while, she thought to herself, it can't do any harm to see whether the story is true. So one night she decided to walk to the pool. It was over a kilometre from where she lived, but so strong was her intention she determined to walk the distance. Alone.

As she approached, she heard the mermaid singing. Even as the sound chilled her to the bone it captivated and drew her to the pool. Dora heard the footsteps and dived into the water leaving the comb behind. The comb was so beautiful it could only belong to a mermaid. Among its finely carved teeth were a few silky strands of the mermaid's green-tinted hair.

Hazel held the comb in her hand and heard the song and the message it gave:

> 'Take my comb
> Return to your home
> And I will come to you in your dream.
> Take my comb
> Return to your home
> And I will give you your heart's desire
> Soo-oo-oooo-ooon.'

Hazel ran home clutching the comb.

On the following night she had barely fallen asleep when Dora appeared in a dream. The mermaid was more beautiful than Hazel could ever have imagined. But Hazel had no time to admire the mermaid's beauty. Her gaze was fastened on the green glory of hair that framed the mermaid's face in gentle waves and flowed softly over her shoulders. It fell below her waist, cascading down until it sheathed the mermaid's fins.

When Dora spoke her voice was soft, sweet and caressing.

'What is your greatest wish, my dear?' she asked.

Hazel, choking with emotion, replied, 'Oh, I would give everything for hair as long and beautiful as yours!'

'This you shall have, my dear,' said Dora. 'Come with me to the pool. Sit on the rock that is my throne. Look down into the water and pass my comb through your hair. The lovely hair you so desire shall be yours.'

And the dream ended.

Hazel awoke at once. There beside her was the mermaid's comb. She snatched it up and was out of bed running to the pool.

When she got there she scrambled on to the rock and, looking down into the water, she began to comb her hair. And each time the pull through was longer. Hazel saw that her hair now reached her neck, tickling it with such strangeness that she felt her blood curdle with cold. Soon her hair was flowing past her shoulders, and it was soft and brown like the tuft of hair at the end of an ear of full-grown corn. Soon it lay in thick tresses round her hips.

And now the rhythm of the combing became a command. 'Comb! Comb! Comb!' And her hands obeyed, combing faster and faster. The hair grew longer and longer. As it grew, her neck bent towards the pool. She saw her hair spreading out on the surface of the water and, as it soaked up water, it sank deeper and deeper, pulling Hazel, pulling, pulling. Down, down, down, she bent until – SPLASH! The hair had dragged her from the rock into the pool. Hazel tried to grab the rock, but her fingers slipped off its mossy green surface. She grasped at empty air, and sank to the bottom.

The next night Dora was back on the rock, combing her hair and singing her wordless haunting melody . . . 'Mmmmmmm mmmm mmmmmmmmmmm . . .'

her hair was flowing past her shoulders and it was soft
and brown like the fur of ... and she could almost felt
... warm ... how it lay on her shoulders round her hips.

And now the rhythm of the song ... became a
creature. Came down towards ... and looking down
... faster. The hair grew longer and
... as it grew, and now bent towards the pool. She
was not now floating out on the surface of the water and
... reached up ... to ... and drown ... reaching
... bare, pulling down, down, down, she felt and
felt ... she turned and dragged her ... the rock and
the pool. Hands tried to grab the rocks against ... figure
slipped off the mossy green surface. She grasped at empty
air and sank to the bottom.

The next night there were rocks on the surface, combing her
hair and singing her wordless, haunting, far-off call.
Maintaining the most constant monotonous ...

The River Muma
Jamaica

Early in the morning, before anyone was stirring, River Muma would leave the water and perch on a rock to sing her sweet, sad songs.

One morning, a young man returning from hunting heard the singing and was drawn to the river. He saw a beautiful woman sitting on a rock combing her long, black hair. The comb was inset with pearls and precious stones.

'River Muma!' he called. 'How you so pretty!'

Surprised, River Muma dropped the comb and dived into the river. The young man picked up the comb and went home. He told no one about the encounter and hid the comb under his pillow.

That night he dreamed of River Muma. In the dream she seemed to be pleading with him to return the comb to her. But when he looked at the comb the next day, and saw how brightly the stones glowed, he thought of all the pleasures he could provide for his wife with the money the comb would bring. He put it back under his pillow. Still he told his wife nothing.

He had no sooner fallen asleep that night when he dreamed about River Muma. This time she was singing and the sadness in her voice so touched his heart that he was determined to return the comb to her the following day. On his way to the river he met his aged mother who was a widow. He was her only means of support. When he thought of what might become of her if anything should happen to him, he turned back. A small portion of what he would get for the jewels alone, would provide for his mother until she died.

'River Muma don't need gold nor jewels, and the river has enough gold to make her as many combs as she want,' he said to himself.

He would hide the comb until he could find a merchant who would pay him a good price for it.

The young man did not go to the forest that day but lay in bed thinking about the comb and what River Muma might do to him. He knew that she could put a spell on him with a song that would draw him to the river. Then she would drown him. And if a man vexed her she would follow him everywhere he went. He would not be able to eat, he would not be able to sleep. In the end he would go mad. But he had also heard say that if you found River Muma's comb, she might tell you how to get gold and riches.

That night he was afraid to go to sleep. Afraid of what he might see and hear in his dream. But no sooner had he fallen asleep than River Muma began to sing. The song she sang was so full of anguish that it startled the young man awake. He rose from his bed and silently crept from the house so as not to awaken his wife. He headed straight for the river. As he neared the river he heard the Muma singing and trembled. It was the same song he had heard in his dream. He wanted to run away from that place, from that song, from River Muma, but he could not. He ran towards the river and as he ran he called, 'I comin' River Muma! I comin' to bring back your comb!'

He threw the comb far into the river and heard the splash as it hit the water. When the ripples subsided the singing stopped, and for a moment all was quiet.

The young man returned home.

Early next morning he set out for the forest to hunt. At the foot of the rock where he first saw River Muma, there was a heap of gold coins glinting in the sunlight. He gathered them up and put them in his hunting bag. When he returned home he told his wife all that had happened since he first saw River Muma, but he said to her, 'You must never speak of this or we will lose everything.'

And to this day no one knows how they became the wealthiest family in the district.

An Undersea Adventure
Trinidad & Tobago

There was, on the island of Tobago, a young woman called Margaret. She was the village beauty and an excellent swimmer. One day, as she was swimming in the sea, a man suddenly appeared beside her. He was young and soft-spoken and soon the two were chatting like old friends. After a while, the young man said, 'Margaret, there are some lovely underwater gardens not far away. You would have to be a strong swimmer though. How good a swimmer are you?'

The young woman was taken aback when he spoke her name, for she had not told it to him. However, she replied, 'I've been told that I'm like a fish in water.'

'Then you have no fear of the sea?' he enquired.

'I fear the sea as much as I fear the land. No more, no less,' she said.

'Well, let's see what kind of fish you are,' he teased.

41

And, seizing her hand, he dived so swiftly that, before she knew it, she was in a large hall with walls of coral festooned with sea-green vines. The rooms which led off from the hall were a sight to behold, and were paved with marble floors that shone like glass.

Margaret saw her companion fully for the first time. He was no mortal but a merman. Yet she was not afraid of him, for he continued to treat her with courtesy. She herself was curious about everything and fascinated by the spectacular gardens in which there were flowering shrubs of coral which mirrored many that grew on land. There was so much to see that Margaret was surprised when the merman said to her, 'You have been here for three days. Would you like to stay and be my true companion?'

'Three days! Why, I thought I'd been here only a few hours. How is it that I've neither eaten nor slept yet feel none the worse for it?' she asked.

'Time feels different undersea because of the flow of water and also because there are no changes of day and night. But tell me, Margaret, will you stay?'

She didn't know what to do or say. To tell the truth she was in love with this gentle man of the sea, but to stay with him meant that she would never see her family and friends again. She was clever enough though, not to provoke his anger with a hasty refusal.

'Let me think about it for a little longer,' she begged.

Now that Margaret knew he wanted her to stay she was careful about what she ate and drank. She had heard that water beings could bewitch a person by giving them certain food and drink. So she drank only clear fresh water and ate only sea grapes. Finally she told the merman that she wished to return to her world. 'I am likely to die from homesickness if I cannot see my world and my own folk, even though I am enchanted by your world and I care about you.'

And since he loved her truly he let her go, taking her up through a tunnel to the beach nearest her village.

Before they parted he gave her two things. One was a beautiful conch shell, which she should blow should she ever need him. The other was a stone which reflected the colours of the rainbow when it was held up to the sun.

'This is a special stone only found deep under the sea,' said the merman. 'It will ensure a long life, and good fortune will be with you always.'

And so it was. Margaret lived to be one hundred years and she never lost her beauty. She never moved from her village near the sea. When she died she was buried at sea, as she wished.

Mr Noel
Trinidad

Once upon a time people believed that to fish during Holy Week was to invite the hostility of the spirits of river and sea. Perhaps there are some who still hold that belief. Whether so or not, Mr Noel was not one of them and no one could persuade him to leave off fishing in that particular week.

'If it's safe to eat fish on Good Friday, then it's safe to catch fish in the week of Good Friday,' replied Mr Noel when he was warned about the fishing. And off he went to the river to set his nets and traps.

From Sunday to Wednesday of Holy Week he caught many different kinds of fish. He caught so much that for once his basket was filled to overflowing. On Thursday he set out for his village, carrying on his head the basket brim-full of fish. He had not travelled a kilometre from the river when he heard a strange sound behind him. He looked back. What he saw filled him with such horror that he stopped dead in his tracks.

An enormous, white horse was galloping through the woods with a creature, half woman, half serpent, perched on its back. Her long, tawny tresses streamed out behind her as she urged the horse onwards with her serpent-like tail.

'*Tonné*! *C'est Mama Dlo*!' cried Mr Noel and he took to his heels. But no matter how fast he ran he heard the clip-clop of the horse's hooves and the slip-slap of the serpent's tail on the horse's shanks and his heart felt fit to burst. He knew the basket of fish was holding him back for it was heavy but Mr Noel could not bear to lose *all* his fish. Besides, he knew how his friends would gloat over his misfortune. So he threw out a third of the fish to lighten his load.

When Mama Dlo saw him do this she called out:

'Fish or no fish I go catch you man,
Fish or no fish I go whup you man,
You come in me water,
Me Children you slaughter
Every week in the year.
You too greedy man!'

And with that the horse made a spurt which narrowed the

distance between man and beast. Mr Noel heard the threat and soon felt the breath of the horse close behind. Suddenly Mr Noel saw that they were coming to another river. He did not dally any longer with the basket of fish but threw all his remaining catch – and the last of his pride – to the winds and plunged into the water just ahead of the horse. Mama Dlo could not enter any other river but her own. As he swam across the wide wide stream she called out to him from the bank, 'Ho! Man, you get away from me but you better watch out because there's a Mama just like me in that river.'

Mr Noel was still in danger. A serpent woman of any river could smell a human being very quickly, especially if that human carried the taint of fish. With the warning of Mama Dlo ringing in his head, Mr Noel strained every muscle to reach the safety of the far side before he was caught.

He was within leaping distance of the other bank when he heard a whistling sound and felt a stinging lash across his back. Whack! Even through his oilskin jerkin the blow was so powerful that Mr Noel shot out of the water like a flying fish and landed on the river's edge. He was bent double with pain from the whiplash of the second Mama's tail. Another lash would have cut him in half; but she could come no further for at Mr Noel's back was a small village church with a cross rising above the door.

As soon as Mr Noel could stand he went into the church to say a prayer of thanksgiving for his life. And ever since that day no one can persuade Mr Noel to go fishing in river or in sea at *any* time of the year.

Nothing but a Pair
of Shoes

Trinidad & Tobago

In a village by a river there lived a boy called Thomasos. Long before he could walk he would crawl down to the river to gaze at the silver fish swimming in the sunlit water. Thomasos grew into an open-natured youth, but in his eighteenth year a change came over him. He became secretive and hardly spoke to anyone. One by one his friends left him. All but a girl named Rosa, who had loved Thomasos since they were children. She was sure that Thomasos was courting a girl from another village, so one evening she followed him down to the river.

Rosa saw him sit down on a boulder, remove his shoes and roll up his trouser legs. She hid behind a hedge and waited to see what would happen.

The sun was sinking on the horizon, leaving a trail of

gold, orange and red streaks across the sky. Suddenly, there was a ripple on the water and in the middle of the river, a head emerged. Rosa saw a woman whose hair fell in thick, black tresses down her back and gleamed blue in the glow of the setting sun. She seemed to be gliding along and when she drew near the bank, Thomasos waded into the water to meet her. They embraced and arm in arm headed towards the boulder. It was then Rosa saw something that shocked her. This was no mortal woman but a fairymaid!

Rosa's brain was in turmoil because fairymaids and mermaids were known to be the most fiendish of supernatural beings, for they robbed humans of their souls.

When Rosa arrived at Thomasos's house she was in such a state that all she could do was to rock back and forth.

'Rosa child, tell us what is the matter?' begged Thomasos's mother.

It was some time before the girl was calm enough to speak. 'Thomasos is in love with a fairymaid. I just see them by the river,' she sobbed.

The mother ran to the windows and shut and latched them. Then she whispered, 'For the love of God, don't speak so loud. You sure this is truth?'

'Yes, yes! I see them from the hedge. Come, see for yo'self if you don't believe me.'

It was a bitter truth for Thomasos's parents to accept,

but they did not really doubt the girl's story. She was too distressed.

'That boy been acting strange for a long time,' said the father, 'but I never thought to see the day when such a thing could happen to a child of mine.'

'What will you do to save him?' asked Rosa.

'Listen now, Rosa, you keep silent about what you see tonight or *your* life will be in danger,' advised the father. 'We will try to get help for the boy.'

The following day Thomasos's father consulted a man well-versed in secret rituals, known as John the Workman. Two days later John found the place where Rosa had hidden when she spied on the fairymaid and Thomasos. The hedge was high up on the bank yet close enough to see what took place.

After a few nights of watching John went to see the boy's parents to tell them what he had observed and what had to be done.

'There is hope for the boy,' he said. 'He still has his shadow though it is faint. The moment he loses that, the fairymaid will have robbed him of his soul. No one can save him then.'

When the parents heard this the mother wept and the father asked, 'What can you do to save our son?'

'What I have in mind will be dangerous for the lad. You must be patient and trust me,' said John.

'We will do whatever you think best,' the father replied.

'The first thing you must do is to impress on your son that if he does not break with the creature at once he will lose his soul. When you have done that we will make plans.'

When Thomasos returned home that evening his mother told him all she knew about his secret meetings with the fairymaid but he said nothing.

'Speak to me, Thomasos!' she pleaded. 'This is dangerous business for all the people who love you.' The boy remained silent.

His mother was caught between anger and desperation. She did not know how to reach her son. Then she remembered how close he was to his grandmother when she was alive.

'If you allow this creature to destroy your soul, how will the spirit of your grandmother find peace?' she asked.

Then Thomasos broke down and wept.

'Ma, I tried to break away from the maid, but she threaten to hurt you and Pa. And now it's too late for me!'

'No, son, it's not too late. We have someone here who can help you. His name is John and he's a wise old man. If anyone can free you, he can. Will you allow him to help you, Thomasos?'

'I'll try, Ma. Gran will help me.' Thomasos promised.

On the same night Thomasos and the Workman went to

the river. John held a stick with carvings on it. Thomasos wore a pair of new shoes. It had been difficult for John to persuade the parents to remain at home but they agreed because they trusted him.

'This is something Thomasos must do on his own. If you are present the maid will believe that his will is weak and he will never be free of her,' said John.

'But you will be with the lad. Will she not think the same?' asked the father.

'No,' replied John. 'I am here as a go-between to bargain with her for the boy's soul. She will understand what that means.'

'John, you have to do more than bargain. You have to protect him,' insisted the mother. 'The boy so full of fear I don't know if he has the will to stand against that demon. And she mean to have him.'

'It's true that once a fairymaid set her heart on a human lover she will do everything in her power to rid him of his soul. But the maid have to get past my power first. Have faith in your son.'

As the moon rose over the river the fairymaid came gliding through the water to the place where Thomasos sat. John was hidden behind the boulder. At the sight of the fairymaid Thomasos forgot his promise and tried to go and meet her, but the Workman was prepared. He gripped the boy's legs and held him fast. The fairymaid wondered at her lover's stillness but came gliding on. When she was near, Thomasos stretched out his arms to hold her. Instantly, John was out of his hiding place. He grabbed her and wound her tresses around the magic stick he carried. The stick would curb her power. Then he dragged her out of the water, but she threw a comb to Thomasos.

'Throw the comb in the river,' she shouted.

'No! No! Give it to me!' commanded the Workman.

'If you love me, Thomasos, throw it in the river,' she pleaded.

Thomasos could not help himself. He threw the comb into the river.

Immediately he did so, the fairymaid changed into a cat, sprang from the Workman's grasp and leaped into the river.

'Oh, Thomasos!' cried the Workman. 'Why did you disobey my order? There is only one thing to do now. You must call her up from the river.'

Thomasos looked at the Workman in surprise. 'Call her up! But after what happened surely she will not return!'

'Oh, yes!' declared John. 'She won't give up so easily and, besides, she has a score to settle. She will return, but only you can call her up.'

'Tell me what to do. I promise on my grandmother's grave that I will do it!' So the Workman gave Thomasos a secret word and told him what he must do. He stayed close to the boy, but did not touch him. He could not interfere until Thomasos had done his part.

The boy spoke the word and the water parted. The fairymaid appeared. She came near enough to the bank so that Thomasos could see her beauty, but this time she stayed out of his reach. Then she stretched out her arms and cried, 'Thomasos, even if you no longer love me, give me one last kiss that I may remember the love we once shared.'

He was so moved by her tone of despair that he would have gone to her, but just then he heard the cry of a cat in the distance. He remembered what had taken place earlier that night, and the promise he had made to the Workman. He turned away from her.

Now he was joined by John. 'What payment will you take to free this mortal?' John asked the fairymaid.

'Nothing you can offer will pay for the love you have destroyed. I would rather see him dead.' She was no longer beautiful and soft-spoken. Her face was ugly with malice and her voice harsh with hate.

'Perhaps so,' said John, 'but I have something which will weaken your power if you harm him.' And opening his hand he showed what lay there.

Her eyes widened with surprise as she gazed at three strands of her hair.

'What will you give me to free him?' she asked in a

voice as cold as the stones that lay at the bottom of the river.

'Nothing but a pair of shoes and three strands of your hair,' replied John who gave them to her. And so it was that, as moon was catching day, Thomasos was set free from the fairymaid's enchantment.

He never wore shoes after that night! After all it was *his* pair of shoes the fairymaid took away. Who knows what she might do to a pair of shoes to draw him back to her!

Oriyu and the Fisherman
An Arawak legend, South America

A man went out in his corial to fish.

Suddenly he felt something tug at his hook. He tried to pull in the line but couldn't draw it in. Then he tried again pulling with all his might. Slowly the line began to move out of the water, until he was able to see what he had caught.

It was Oriyu herself! Oriyu, the spirit and guardian of the river, with her hair all entangled in the hook. The man hoisted her into his boat and wasted no time rowing back to the bank. When they arrived at his dwelling, and his mother saw the woman, she was dumbstruck, for she knew at once who it was.

Then Oriyu spoke for the first time to the fisherman, 'I will remain with you and be your wife, but you must make me a promise.'

'Tell me what you wish me to do,' he said.

'Neither you nor your mother must ever tell anyone who I am or I shall have to return to my home in the river.'

And the man and his mother promised.

Oriyu was a good wife and helpmate to her husband. When they went fishing she would show him where the fish was plentiful, for her keen eyes could pierce the muddy river water. Time after time they returned home, their boat laden with fish. And Oriyu gave generously to those whose catch was poor and were without food.

The people wondered at the sudden arrival of such a beautiful woman, and the good fortune of the fisherman. On a certain night all the people came together for a celebration. The fisherman's mother drank freely of a powerful drink which excited the senses and loosened her tongue. She let out her daughter-in-law's secret. At once the story spread like wildfire, and eventually reached Oriyu's ears. She thought her husband had betrayed her trust and was much grieved.

'I have brought you good fortune yet you repay me by breaking your word!' she accused him.

But her husband protested saying, 'I told no one how you came to be here or who you are.' And looking into his eyes she knew that he spoke the truth.

They confronted his mother, who confessed that it was she who had revealed the secret, and begged Oriyu's forgiveness. The old woman was truly repentant. She knew how much they owed to Oriyu, who had made life so comfortable for them. Oriyu forgave the old woman, but the damage was done. She would have to return to the river.

At last a time came when everyone had forgotten the incident. The fish were leaping in the river, the crabs were crowding on to the land. Then Oriyu said to her husband, 'Tell your mother to invite some of her friends to accompany us on a fishing trip.'

So a party of people got into the fisherman's corial and set out. When they were in the middle of the river where the water is deepest, Oriyu said to her husband, 'During all our years together, you have never met my people. Let us pay them a visit!'

They told the others they would soon return to the boat and Oriyu and the fisherman dived into the water.

The fisherman's mother was beginning to worry about their long absence, when one of Oriyu's sisters appeared with a net full of fish. She also brought a basket of vegetables which no one had seen before.

'My sister and her husband send you these gifts. They say that you must return to your homes and plant the vegetables at once. Tend them well and they will yield food for all the people.' And she dived into the water.

Sad at heart the mother and her friends sailed back to land. The mother often returned to the river where her son had disappeared, and called to him. She never saw him again.

The Arawak tribe planted the vegetables, which they called cassava. Later they learned to make a drink from it called cassiri. They drink this when they hold celebrations of song and dance and telling stories.

The Mermaid of the Lake
Wales

Everyday when Bryn took his flock of sheep to graze he used to sit near the lake Llyn-y-Fan Fach. He would play such lively tunes on his flute that the sheep would leap and gambol on the grassy slopes of the Black Mountains of Carmarthenshire. As he was playing his flute one day Bryn saw a young woman on the far side of the lake. He was so surprised that he stopped playing.

'Bryn,' she called, 'will you play another tune for me?'

Her voice was as sweet and clear as the tone of his flute. The boy put his lips to the pipe and the air was filled with music so merry that the sheep and their lambs skipped and frolicked all the way down the grassy slopes to the lake. And if the music hadn't stopped, they would have danced into the lake and joined the lass as she came across the lake, sometimes swimming and sometimes dancing.

She was a mermaid and her fish tail fanned out behind

her and the scales shimmered and sparkled as they caught the light. Her jet-black hair, rippling down her back, was in striking contrast to her milk-white skin and her bright blue eyes.

Bryn had never seen such beauty. He didn't know what to say to her for he knew nothing about girls and the words that please them. He knew only that he wanted to be close to her and to touch her.

One of the sheep was nuzzling at the lunch bag his mam filled with barley loaves and cheese every day. So Bryn took out three loaves and offered them to the mermaid. 'Will you share some bread with me?'

But the girl tossed her head and said:

'Hard-baked is thy bread
You won't catch me so easy.'

With that she dived into the water and disappeared.

That night Bryn told his mother about the mermaid and what she said about the bread.

'Since her taste is not for bread well-baked I will not bake tomorrow's loaves,' said his mam.

On the following day Bryn went as usual to the lake and sat playing his flute, but he kept his eyes on the water hoping to see the mermaid. He waited as the sun climbed high in the sky and began its descent and then, there she was in the middle of the lake.

Bryn was all a-fluster at her sudden appearance. And she was floating across the water towards him! What was the poor lad to do? He reached into his bag and took out three loaves, which he offered to her.

'Me mam prepared these especially for you,' he said.

She looked kindly at him and smiled but she said:

> 'Unbaked is thy bread
> You won't catch me so easy.'

And so saying she dived into the lake and was gone from sight.

Bryn was so bedazzled by the mermaid's smile that he hardly noticed her departure. He rounded up his animals and went home.

'Well, did your maid like the bread?' enquired his mother.

'No, Mam, she said it wasn't baked and refused it.'

His mother saw how brightly his eyes shone and heard how his voice trembled when he spoke of the mermaid, and she thought it more than likely he'd fallen in love with the lass. She said no more about it but decided she would not bake that night but leave it until morning so that the loaves would be not too hard nor yet too soft.

At the first crowing of the cock Bryn was up. As soon

as the bread was baked he was off with the flock of sheep to the lake Llyn-y-Fan Fach.

All day he waited and watched. The sun's light was beginning to fade and Bryn was thinking of gathering his sheep, when some cows appeared in the middle of the lake, and with them the mermaid. Bryn wasted no time offering her the barley loaves, which were not too hard nor yet too soft. This time the mermaid accepted them for they were just right.

Then the two of them sat for a long while talking about this and that, and finally Bryn asked her to become his wife. She agreed without any fuss but she warned, 'Bryn, I will live with you on land and be your wife until the day you touch me with iron. Remember that iron is harmful to some of us from the Other World.' Bryn promised never to touch her with iron.

The mermaid's father offered a dowry from his vast stock of animals beneath the water.

'You may have as many animals as my daughter can count on one breath,' he said to the couple.

The maid was clever and had learned to hold her breath from living under the water. She managed to count in fives as the animals came out of the water – cows, goats, pigs, sheep, horses – so the couple were now rich.

Bryn and his mermaid were married, and in time they had three sons.

All went well until one day when Bryn and his wife attended a christening. In the midst of the rejoicing and festivities, Bryn's wife burst into tears. The hosts were taken aback at her outburst and wanted to know what ailed her. 'We should mourn at a christening and rejoice at a funeral,' she said. 'Birth is the beginning of man's pain and sorrow while death is a happy release.' And she continued to weep so loudly that eventually Bryn had to take her home.

When they got back, Bryn, who was still annoyed with his wife, removed the bridle from the horse and threw it at her.

'You put that away in the stable. I'll take the horse to graze in the fields,' he said.

As she caught it, the iron of the bridle touched her hand.

'Oh Bryn!' she cried out. 'Iron has destroyed our happiness. I must now return to the lake. I cannot remain on land.'

At once she went to the farmyard and called all the animals she had brought with her from the bottom of the lake – the cows, the goats, the pigs, the sheep, even the horse her husband was about to take to the field – and led them back to the lake Llyn-y-Fan Fach. In a thrice they disappeared.

Too late Bryn realised what his anger had caused. He was distraught with grief and guilt. That same night, when everyone was asleep, he left the house and walked straight into the lake, into the deepest part, until the water covered him and he sank to the bottom.

The boys were now orphans, so their grandmother came to look after them, but every day they would walk besides the lake hoping they might see their mother. One day they did. She comforted them and promised that she would come from beneath the water whenever they called. Each time they met she taught them the names of the plants growing near the lake.

'Some of these plants are herbs which will heal the sick,' she said, 'but you must learn how to brew the herbs, and what each herb will heal.' So she taught her boys how to make medicines and potions from herbs and flowers.

When the boys grew up, they opened a shop where they sold herbs and medicines and their reputation as healers spread far beyond the borders of Carmarthenshire. Soon they earned enough money to study medicine at university.

It has been said that they were among the first people to qualify as doctors in Wales and that many of their descendants became famous physicians.

Part Two

Sea Monsters

How Fox Tricked the Leviathan

When the Lord of the Universe created planet Earth, he filled it with his creatures. And the land was alive with sounds, colours and movement. But in the waters there was only the ebb and flow of tides, the ripple and rush of rivers and streams.

'My Lord,' said his attendant, 'in all your works you are indeed All-mighty, but in the matter of this creation you are not all-finished.'

'What then is amiss?' was the Lord's retort. He was more than a little piqued at this unexpected criticism.

'While creatures abound in air and on land, you have created none for the sea,' said the attendant.

'I have made all that is needed here on Earth,' insisted the Lord. 'So go now, take one pair of each family – male and female – and place them in the ocean.' He had laboured for six days and nights without rest. He was determined to take some time off for meditation.

It was done as he commanded. Joyfully the creatures took to the water. All except Fox.

The ruler over all the creatures that dwelt in the sea, was a monster of great magnitude. He was called the Leviathan. He held a gathering to meet his subjects and noticed that one creature was missing.

'Why is the Fox creature not present?' he enquired.

'O Great Ruler, Fox is the cleverest of all creatures on land,' said Catfish, 'for he is the only one who has not been placed in the water.'

'How did that happen?' asked the Leviathan.

'When the attendant of the Mighty One sought to place the Fox family in the sea, that clever creature leaned far over the water so that his body was reflected. "There is a Fox already in the water," he said to the attendant, who believed him.'

Now the Leviathan considered himself to be not just lord of the waters but also the wisest of all beings. So he was not at all pleased to learn that there was such a clever creature on land. He said to two large dolphins, 'Go and fetch this Fox creature. Bring him to me so that I might test his wisdom.'

Of course he meant to kill Fox and eat him. Thus Fox would be destroyed and his cunning added to the Leviathan's.

When the dolphins got close to the shore they saw a four-legged creature with a long bushy tail sitting high up on a mound overlooking the sea. They called to him, 'Where can we find the creature known as Fox?'

'Why do you seek him?' asked Fox. He was as cautious as he was cunning. The dolphins had sensed the Leviathan's real reason for wanting Fox brought before him, but they said, 'Our great king is very old and close to death. He has heard of the cunning and cleverness of Fox and intends that he should succeed him as ruler of the sea kingdom.'

When Fox heard this, his heart within him leaped for joy. He thought to himself, day after day I must hunt for my food risking danger from fierce beasts, not to mention those that swoop from the sky. If what these creatures say is true, then my life will be free from all fears. What is more I shall be surrounded by great luxury with servants to do my every bidding!

Still he wanted to be assured. 'Tell me more about this great king and his kingdom.'

'The Leviathan, our king, is the wisest of all creatures and his home is a splendid palace beneath the sea. He dines on the finest morsels and is attended by hundreds of servants. He has but to speak and his word is law.'

'I am Fox and I will come with you. But since I am no water creature how shall I get to the bottom of the sea?'

'Have no fear,' chorused the dolphins. 'We shall transport you safely on our backs. For you must know that we are the king's most trusted messengers and are used to performing this task.'

So Fox climbed on to their backs and swimming close together, the dolphins set forth across the wide ocean.

All went smoothly until they came to a place where the waves were rough and high. Then fear seized Fox's heart and he thought deeply on his plight. What if all was not as the dolphins promised? And if it were not, how would he make his way back to land from the depths of the ocean?

Fox spoke to the dolphins, 'I am now in your power and have no means of escape, so tell me truly why you sought me out.'

The dolphins, who no longer saw the need to keep up the pretence, said, 'The truth is that the Leviathan is well and strong, and we believe that he envies your cunning and intends to destroy you and eat your heart. He believes that it is the source of your cleverness.'

What could Fox do? He called on every iota of cunning to save his life. 'Why did you not tell me this when we first met? It would be an honour to present so great a king with my humble heart. Alas! I fear it is not to be.'

'Not to be!' exclaimed the dolphins in unison. 'But why?'

'Do you suppose that we foxes walk around with our

hearts! That would be both dangerous and foolish.'

'Where then is it kept if not in your body?' asked one of the dolphins.

'That is a secret I cannot divulge, as all foxes take a sacred oath never to reveal the hiding place of our hearts, even on pain of death.'

If only it were possible to take me back to the place where you found me, I could fetch the heart for you,' said Fox.

Well, the dolphins did think that it might be a trick. After all they knew Fox's reputation. On the other hand if it *were* true and they returned without the heart, they knew what their fate would be. The Leviathan did not suffer fools gladly.

The dolphins decided to trust Fox. They turned around and headed for land.

As soon as his feet touched the firm earth Fox barked for joy. He danced and cavorted like a pup as he rejoiced in the pleasure of being on dry land.

'Hurry, Fox! Hurry! Fetch the heart so that we may return to the Leviathan quickly,' called the dolphins.

But Fox said to them, 'Do you suppose I could live without my heart in my body?'

The dolphins realised that Fox had deceived them and they were greatly afraid.

'What shall we tell our king?' they asked tearfully.

'Tell your great ruler that he should have come himself. Tell him if I was able to outsmart the Almighty's attendant, how much easier must it be to outsmart mere messengers of the sea king.' And off he ran far, far from the sea to the great forest in the highlands.

Of course the dolphins were punished for allowing Fox to escape. And the Leviathan raised a storm which swamped the land around the seashore. But Fox was already safe in his hideaway.

Since that time there are creatures in the sea which resemble every creature on land but there is none that looks like Fox.

The Monster in the
Water Hole

Australia

Alchera was a time when all things were as one and there was harmony in nature. In those days of the Dreamtime all beings understood each other and could transform themselves into whatever they wished to be. But as the spirits of the ancestors returned to their resting place there was a change. Some creatures used their strength and swiftness to control others, even to destroy them. They became monsters. Such a creature inhabited a large water hole. It was part goanna, part fish, and had grown enormous from a continuous diet of fish, water snakes, and any land creature that lingered too long in the water or swam too deep. Those who had seen it called it Gannafish.

One day Catman came to the water hole. He was a

clever fisherman who had fashioned many spears from the bamboo grass, sharpening each to a fine point, then binding them together. With this weapon he was able to spike many fish and fatally wound them. He could also chant spells which brought the fish swarming into his nets.

Catman lay on the ground above the pool gazing down. His eyes penetrated the water to the black depths where the creature rested.

'Eeeh!' Catman cried. 'To trap such a creature would make a good feast for all the tribe.'

At once he left for the ancestral grounds to perform rituals that would strengthen his magic, and to weave a net of vines which could hold such a large beast. As he was returning to the water hole, he met men from another tribe.

'Hai!' he greeted them. 'A large monster lies at the bottom of the pool. Come fish with me and we will share the catch.'

'The monster you speak of is Gannafish. It is his ancestors that formed the hole and sang the rain to fill it with water. Do not disturb him lest he destroy you,' warned an old man. Catman continued on his way.

When he arrived at the pool he again peered into the water. The monster was lying in the same spot where Catman had first seen it.

'Ah, Gannafish! Let others stay on land and catch crabs.

I fish in deep waters.' He began to chant the spell to call the monster up from the deep, and Gannafish trembled when he heard the chanting. Then slowly he swam upwards, his eyes closed, his capacious mouth gaping wide. The sun's light beamed through the water, and halfway up Gannafish felt its warmth. He opened his eyes and saw where he was heading. He heard the chanting and felt the old magic drawing him. He struggled to escape the drowsiness that threatened to overpower him, thrashing about in an effort to escape.

Meanwhile Catman was beginning to tire, and as the power of the magic waned, Gannafish broke free and dived swiftly down to the safety of darkness at the bottom of the pool.

Night fell and Catman made camp near the hole. He wanted to start fishing as the new day dawned. At that time the magic power would be strong enough to bring the monster close to the surface, where Catman could spear him. That night while Catman slept and dreamed of conquest, Gannafish was in turmoil. All his instincts warned him to flee from the pool, from a familiar place where he had never known danger, and where there was always food in abundance. Round and round he swam churning up the soft sand at the bottom. Fear swelled in him, and he charged at the walls surrounding the pool bed, which now seemed to imprison him. His massive head battered through the earth and rock, and he burrowed further and further inland. His powerful tail brushed aside falling rubble, clearing a path for the water, which flowed in his wake from the pool.

By the time Catman awoke he saw a swift-flowing river where, just the day before, there had been land. It stretched far away, beyond sight. There was no sign of Gannafish in the pool, only swirling muddy water.

'So Gannafish runs! But he can't hide from me. I will track him until he is caught in my net or hooked on my spear,' boasted Catman.

Catman ran hard and fast following the course of the river. All day he ran until he came to a place where the water was trapped in an underground cave. He walked softly so as not to disturb Gannafish. Quietly he removed the earth at the top of the cave until he had made a large hole. Then, with one quick plunge, he thrust his spear down on to the monster's back. But the hard scales protected the creature's body. The spear glanced off its back.

Now Gannafish was wild with rage that he should be so pursued and attacked. He smashed through the cave scattering everything in his path, and bit through interlocking tree roots, deeply buried in the earth. He meandered and plunged, cleaving the earth, creating ravines down mountain sides, and forming subterranean rivers which still exist today. He snatched land creatures from their pastures and devoured them as he fled.

Catman's wives and children were searching among the rocks and tide-pools for crabs and eels and shellfish when they heard a thunderous sound. What they saw filled them with such terror that they abandoned all their much-needed food and scrambled to the top of the highest rock. The strangest creature they had ever seen was gliding at great speed towards them. It looked like a giant goanna with the pointed face of a crocodile. Layers of black shiny scales covered part of its back and translucent scales covered the lower part of its body, which formed a broad fish tail. It was the length of two men and twice as broad.

Even though they were high up they could feel the ground beneath shaking as the beast approached.

Following close behind, holding his spears and net, was Catman.

One of his wives called to him, 'Stay with us, Catman. We have no one to protect us.'

Their voices stirred a memory in the monster of a dark, quiet place in the water. Now he was being pursued and there was no place he could rest. His large round eyes turned red and his tail twitched furiously. He looked up and saw creatures atop the rock and tried to reach up to where they were cowering. Catman saw the danger his family faced and shouted to distract the monster. Rushing on him before he could turn about, Catman threw one of his wooden spears into the side where there were no scales. But the beast's broad tail swept Catman off his feet. He got up quickly but Gannafish came at him, ready to tear him apart with his sharp teeth. Just before Gannafish leaped, Catman threw another spear at his soft underside and wounded him again. Even though blood was spurting from his wounds, the monster shook off the spear and charged Catman. Back and forth they fought, each wounding the other, yet the struggle continued.

Soon night would descend.

Catman's wives shouted, 'Catman, join us while you can. You cannot kill him, he is too strong.'

His children threw large stones at the monster to chase him away from their father. But neither wives nor children dared to leave the safety of the cliff top to go to Catman's assistance.

Catman saw Diverbird wheeling overhead. He had been following the chase. He said to Catman, 'Gannafish has gone into a pool sheltered by two huge rocks. You cannot follow him there, it is too narrow. He will rest tonight. What will you do?'

'Help me,' begged Catman. 'You and I together, we can bring him down!'

Diverbird said, 'I will do what I can to help.'

He flew in the direction of the rocks where Gannafish was hiding and dived into the water.

Catman waited.

As time passed he grew more anxious for Diverbird's safety. In the dark it would be too dangerous for him to venture near to the wounded beast. He waited through the night, and early in the morning he heard the flurry of wings. Diverbird alighted close to him holding something in his beak. He placed it on the ground before Catman.

'Here is a piece of Gannafish. It is all I could carry in my beak,' said Diverbird.

'Is he dead then?' asked Catman.

'He is not dead though there is much blood from his wounds. But he is deep, deep down and it may be that he will never come up again.'

So Catman gave half of the piece of the monster's body to Diverbird and said, 'You must share this with me for it comes from a creature with a brave heart. From today I will honour you as a hero and my true friend.'

Since that day the people of Catman's tribe have been friend and protector of Diverbird. And what of Gannafish? No one has seen or heard of him since that time. It is possible that he died. Then again, he may just have found a deep, dark place where he feels safe, and where there is food in abundance.

The Snake
Bridegroom: a riddle

West Africa

There was once a chief who had a daughter more beautiful than any woman who lived. Men came from the North and from the South, from the East and from the West to ask, no to beg, for her hand in marriage. But the girl was as arrogant as she was beautiful, and she would have none of them.

The chief's wife had died and his daughter was everything to him. He longed to have the Great House filled with grandchildren, and often pleaded with the girl to choose one of the many admirable young men who came to court her. But she said, 'When I find a man who is wise enough to teach me what I do not already know, I will marry.' And that was an end to it.

Some distance away from the village where the girl

lived there was a freshwater lake which was said to be so deep that no one could measure it. In this lake dwelt a python of awesome size and strength. From the bottom of the lake, the snake often saw the chief's daughter bathing. He heard the girls from the village gossiping as they washed their clothes, about the proud girl who refused to marry. And he decided that he would win the love of the chief's daughter.

So the python transformed himself into a young man and, wrapping a kente cloth around him, he made his way to the village.

It happened that the chief's daughter was going to the lake to bathe and she saw the young man entering the village. At first sight she was smitten with love for the handsome stranger. She returned home and went straight to her father.

'I have seen the man I love and wish to marry,' she announced.

Her father was astounded but hid his surprise as best he could.

'Who is the man and why have you not presented him to me?' he asked.

'I don't know who he is or where he comes from. He has just entered the village,' she replied.

The chief was stunned that his daughter could suggest such an impropriety.

'You wish to marry a man who is unknown to us! A man not of our tribe! I cannot agree to what you ask.'

'Whether you agree or not, I will marry him or I will marry no one.' And nothing the chief or his counsellors said would alter her decision.

When the chief saw that his daughter would not be moved, he sent for the young man, who came at once. He was courteous and treated all who questioned him with respect. But in the end they had to admit that they were none the wiser about who he was. However, he was a personable and clever young man, so the chief put his best face on the matter and gave his consent to the union.

Now, it was the custom for two people about to be married to spend the night before their wedding in a small house away from everyone. This would help them to get to know each other before taking the final step. And so it was done. But during the night, the young man changed back into a python, licked the girl all over, and swallowed her whole. Then, under cover of darkness, he crawled away to his home in the lake.

Early next morning the chief went to bring the betrothed to the Great House where the union would be blessed, and a splendid feast held in their honour. He found the house empty. He looked outside the house thinking the two might be enjoying a walk, but there was no sign of them. Immediately he called on his trackers to search every corner of the land for his daughter and her betrothed. They found no trace of them.

On that same day, an old man came to the chief and said, 'In the days of my grandfather there was a man who could track any creature, man or beast, no matter how long a time had passed.'

The chief said, 'Let that man be brought!'

The man was brought and he led the chief and his followers to the edge of the lake. Then he departed for he had done his part.

As far as they could see there were no bodies floating on the water. None of the men could dive so they were unable to see what lay at the bottom of the lake.

The chief was about to leave when the old man came to him and said, 'Oh chief, in the days of my grandfather there was a man whose thirst was so great that it could never be quenched!'

The chief said, 'Let that man be brought!'

The man was brought, and he knelt beside the lake and drank up all the water. There was only soft brown sand at the bottom.

The chief was filled with despair, yet he would not give up the search. Again, the old man came to him and said, 'Oh my chief, in the days of my grandfather there was a man whose arms could stretch beyond the boundary of our land!'

The chief said, 'Let that man be brought!'

When the man arrived, he extended his right arm down to the sandy bed of the lake and, to his surprise, found the middle portion hollow. He cleared the earth away and saw a large round hole. He reached far, far down into the hole and, after some time, began to pull his arm up again. When he brought it out he was holding the tail of a python. It was an enormous snake and was quite sluggish from the meal it had consumed.

The chief's bodyguard took his sword and slashed at the snake. The skin curled away and revealed a human arm. Carefully he cut away more and more of the skin, and saw a human body wedged tightly in the belly of the snake. He prised the body out and laid it on the ground. Then they saw the face of the corpse. It was the body of the chief's daughter!

The chief and all his party were overwhelmed with grief. While they mourned the old man came to the chief and said, 'Oh great chief, in the days of my grandfather there was a man who could bring the dead to life!'

The chief said, 'Let that man be brought!'

The man was brought, and when he saw the girl laid on the ground, dead yet whole, he sat beside her, and after cleansing her face with water from a phial he carried, he kissed her first in the middle of her forehead, then on her closed eyes, and on her mouth. The girl opened her eyes and, seeing her father, she smiled and stretched out her hands to touch him. He lifted her in his strong arms and held her close as tears of joy ran down his face.

It was a joyful procession that made its way back to the village that day. All the people rejoiced that the girl was restored and sang the praises of those who had helped to find her and bring her back to life.

But the question is, 'Who saved the girl's life?'

The Becoming of Sedna
An Inuit Legend

Anguta, a man of importance in the community, had called Grandmother, the Wise One, to see to his wife who was with child.

For a long time the old woman listened, her ear to the woman's abdomen. With deft fingers she probed and prodded.

'Today we will remove the child,' she announced.

'Ah no!' protested the woman. 'It is too long before the time of borning. The little one will not live.'

She was racked with pain yet sought to protect the babe she carried.

'We will use the steaming stones to coax the babe out. You and I will do the rest. All will be well,' Grandmother assured the woman.

She was the one who helped the people at birthing time and dying time. She was Grandmother to all the living.

89

They took the child from its mother that night. The woman was weak from loss of blood, and her body was so damaged she had no milk to give her newborn. With her first breath the child, Avilayok, clamoured to be fed, and continued to do so day and night.

They gave her milk from the reindeer and she thrived on it, growing and growing. She was always hungry, and at first she ate anything her hands could hold. Later on, she devoured any creature she could outrun. On the night Anguta woke to find his daughter trying to tear one of his arms from his body, he felt enormous fear. He summoned Grandmother.

The Wise One looked into Avilayok's eyes and saw such power that she feared for them all. She saw that as long as the girl did not know that power they would be safe. Until that time she must live away from others.

'Build a small snow hut for the girl,' advised Grandmother. 'Let your fiercest dog keep watch so that no one visits her.'

So Anguta set his daughter apart and put one of his sledge dogs to guard her. He was a sturdy creature and fearless, but he did not work well with other dogs. From the moment Avilayok looked Dog in the eye, he did whatever she asked. Yet, still she did not know her power. She refused to eat the fish and oily stews her parents brought her. She wanted only raw red meat. It was Dog who travelled long distances to find the food she craved.

One day the girl's mother came on Avilayok and Dog unawares, and saw them devouring large chunks of raw meat. She saw, too, the power Avilayok had over Dog. What should she do? She told her husband what she had seen.

'It is time that Avilayok was given as wife,' he said. 'She is old enough.' He announced that the man who took his daughter to his snow hut, would receive a handsome dowry.

When the suitors arrived, they were dismayed to find a girl who towered above the tallest of them, and had the stature of a man. Even the laziest of the men were disgusted by the filthy state of her hut. Bones and gristle littered the floor. The men spurned Anguta's offer. Avilayok herself cared nothing for these men. She had Dog, who provided all her needs.

A winter came, one more severe than many that had gone before. Day after day Dog braved the bitterly cold winds and treacherous snow to find food for Avilayok. While Dog was out searching for food, a stranger arrived in a kayak. He went straight to Avilayok's hut. She greeted her visitor and asked why he had come.

'I'm here to see for myself whether it is true that Avilayok is stronger than any man,' he replied in answer to her question.

The girl was flattered and, as she looked at the stranger, she saw what she wanted to see. In her eyes he was a handsome young man with a thick crop of dark, sleek hair, who wore eye-shades made from fish scales. He was dressed in a dark brown parka with a white lining.

He spoke to her of his home high above the sea and of food in plentiful supply. 'If you agree to be my wife you will have every comfort,' he promised.

Avilayok looked around at her small, cold hut and thought of the constant struggle to find food in the long winters. There was no reason to refuse his offer.

They set off, and in her haste to be gone she never once looked back. So she did not see Dog hurrying to the beach. He shouted a warning but she did not hear.

Avilayok's new home was a large room high up a cliff overlooking the sea. Colourful rugs made from feathers covered the floor. Little oil-lamps lit the room making it seem bright and warm. It was the grandest place she had ever seen. 'Tonight our food will be delicious fruits of the land,' said her husband. 'Tomorrow we shall have fresh fruits of the sea.'

By this time Avilayok was so exhausted from the long sea journey, all she wanted was somewhere to sleep.

When she awoke next morning she was startled to see a large bird staring at her. She sprang up, ready to defend herself, but the bird said, 'Don't be afraid, Avilayok. Don't you know who I am?'

Now she saw that it was the stranger who had asked her to be his wife. Without the eye-shades she saw the bright bird eyes. There was no jacket, only brown feathers with a white breast. He was a stormy petrel and the leader of his tribe. He had wanted a human wife and had employed some of the shaman's magic to impress Avilayok. In the morning light she also saw that the room was just an opening, a cave in the face of the cliff. It was cold and gloomy without the lamplight. She knew at once she could not escape from this place without help.

'My father will reward you well if you take me back,' she begged. But Petrel refused. 'I have chosen you as my wife and you must remain here with me,' he said. 'Besides, I have all that I need.'

Each day at dawn the petrels flew off to their fishing waters. In the evening they returned with fish and fruit. Avilayok's demands for meat were ignored. 'It is taboo for our tribe to eat meat,' said her husband. 'You are now of our tribe and must never again eat meat.'

She tried to find animals among the rocky terrain but it was too high up. Strong winds buffeted her at every step and drove her back into the cave. Petrel wives never left their homes during the day and, with no one to talk to, Avilayok was lonely. At first she believed that her father would come to her rescue, but as time passed she realised that he wouldn't know where to look. Her new home was far, far away from the fishing waters of the human beings.

Dog had told Anguta what he had seen. As soon as winter was over, Anguta and his three sons prepared to set sail in search of Avilayok. Dog was determined to go along, and swore that the seabirds had told him where the girl had been taken. Although Anguta did not trust Dog, he agreed to take him along because he knew that Dog loved his daughter. So they put out to sea.

At last, after a rough journey, they saw the cliffs looming. Soon it would be night. Anguta wanted to make for the beach and climb the cliffs under cover of darkness. But Dog said, 'Every morning petrels travel a long way to fish. Let us wait until they leave.' Anguta agreed and they beached the kayak out of sight and waited.

Early next morning they heard the thunderous sound of birds on the wing. When the sound faded they rowed to the beach at the bottom of the cliffs. Then Dog lifted his head and howled.

In the cave Avilayok heard a familiar noise and rushed to the opening. Far beneath she saw Dog and some men in a kayak. She waved and shouted and heard her father's voice calling to her. Hurriedly Avilayok started to climb down the narrow ledges as her father climbed upwards to help his daughter. He carried her to the boat where Dog and her brothers were waiting.

It happened that one of the petrels had not gone fishing that day. He saw the girl leaving and flew off to warn her husband. Immediately the leader and his tribe of petrels set off in pursuit of Avilayok. Dog knew before any of the others that the birds were on their trail. He had picked up the sound of whirring wings. The rowers doubled their efforts when he warned them, but the birds were gaining speed and would soon catch up with the rescue party.

Dog could see their land ahead. He said, 'The petrels are many and we are few. I will swim quickly and bring help.' And he leaped into the sea and swam away. Soon the sky was darkened with the large flock of birds which swooped down over the kayak.

Anguta hid his daughter under a tangle of nets. But her husband's keen bright eyes saw her. He called out, 'Avilayok, my wife, why are you leaving me? What harm have I done you?'

'Why did you not tell me you were wife to him?' asked Anguta.

'He deceived me into thinking he was human,' whispered the girl.

One of the brothers shouted his sister's reply.

'I did not deceive her,' protested the husband. 'She saw what she wanted to see and agreed to be my wife.'

'Is what he says true?' demanded the father.

'He promised me all the food I wished, yet he refused to bring me meat.'

When Anguta saw his daughter's deceit he grew angry with her. 'If you agreed to be Petrel's wife, you belong to him now. You must go back,' he insisted.

'I will not return to that horrible place,' shouted the girl.

When the petrels saw that Avilayok would not return, they flew low over the sea and beat their wings furiously, causing the waves to swell and toss the kayak about. They created such forceful winds with their movements that Anguta and his sons could not steady the kayak.

Anguta said to his daughter, 'You cannot stay here. Your husband and his tribe will drown us all.'

'Then let us all drown,' said the stubborn girl.

So her father pushed her out of the boat into the sea.

When she saw that he intended to leave her in the water, anger exploded in her and suddenly she felt a surge of tremendous power. She grabbed the kayak to pull it down under the water. Her father, seeing what she intended, struck at her hands with the paddle, but her grasp was firm. So he took his hunting knife and stabbed at her fingers until they bled.

As drops of blood fell in the water, they became animals – seals, walruses, whales – which crowded around the kayak. Anguta and his sons were afraid when they saw the strange creatures, and all the boys joined their father in stabbing at Avilayok. But the girl knew her power now and was no longer afraid. She knew that no one could destroy her. The more they stabbed and slashed off her fingers, the stronger she grew. She would not let go her hold of the boat.

For each finger that was cut off and fell into the sea more creatures were formed. There were polar bears, sea lions and a host of monsters who live in the depths of the sea, and are rarely seen today.

Dog returned with men in kayaks. They saw the bloody struggle taking place between the girl and her family. Dog was about to leap into the sea to help Avilayok when he saw her rise up on a gigantic wave and swamp the kayak and all her brothers and her father. They watched the boat swirl around and sink beneath the water. They did not see it dragged down to the bottom of the sea by Avilayok. They though she was drowned. Her husband and his tribe of petrels mourned her death with a keening sound, and Dog howled for the loss of his beloved Avilayok.

But she had gone eagerly and joyously to the land beneath the sea. No longer Avilayok, but Sedna, ruler of the Underworld.

Avilayok had become creator and destroyer.

The people who had gathered on the beach, saw what had happened. One of them asked, 'Grandmother, why did she drown her own father and brothers?' The old woman was silent for a long time. Her eyes had the far-seeing look of one recalling something that happened a long time ago. Finally she spoke.

'She had that power even before she was born. She was devouring the entrails of her own mother while she was still inside the womb. Had we not forced her out she would have destroyed her. It was a fateful sign!'

And none of those present could doubt it.

Cric Crac
Grace Hallworth

A rich collection of tales from the West Indies,
some familiar, some less-known.
Do you know how the stars came into the sky and how
Turtle got a cracked back?
Eight traditional stories of mischief, greed and good
outwitting evil.

*'A book to cherish, and one which professional and
amateur story-tellers will ignore at their peril.'*
Junior Bookshelf

I Want to be an Angel and other Stories
Jamila Gavin

Four children, each with a dream:
Effie desperately wants to be an angel in the school
nativity play, and even more desperately wants to keep
her family together . . .
Ragiv is miserable because his sister has gone back to
India, but he is happy to find real friendship instead . . .
Dawlish Dobson is always helpful, but what's the secret
he is hiding from Edward . . . ?
Jasmine just wants a family to call her own and a friend
to play with . . .

Jamila Gavin writes with warmth and sympathy about
children who belong to two different cultures.

'beautiful, simple and memorable'
Carnegie Judges

Tilly Mint Tales
Berlie Doherty

When Tilly's mum goes out to work, Mrs Hardcastle pops in to look after her. There are two very special things about Mrs Hardcastle. The first is that she's always dropping off to sleep. The second is that, when she does, something magical happens to Tilly Mint . . .

Tilly visits the island of dreams . . .
learns not to be afraid . . .
and she rides on the owl's back to the stars that sing.

Scary Stories
Edited by Valerie Bierman

A collection of stories which get scarier as you read the book!
Squirm worms under the pavement, and a terrifying old lady who hides in the wardrobe are just some of the characters which are guaranteed to send shivers down your spine . . .

From the best story-tellers:
Julie Bertagna, Malorie Blackman, Terrance Dicks, Vivian French, Julia Jarman, Bel Mooney and Robert Swindells.

A Selected List of Fiction from Mammoth

While every effort is made to keep prices low, it is sometimes necessary to increase prices at short notice . Mandarin Paperbacks reserves the right to show new retail prices on covers which may differ from those previously advertised in the text or elsewhere.

The prices shown below were correct at the time of going to press.

☐ 7497 1421 2	**Betsey Biggalow is Here!**	Malorie Blackman	£2.99
☐ 7497 0366 0	**Dilly The Dinosaur**	Tony Bradman	£3.50
☐ 7497 0137 4	**Flat Stanley**	Jeff Brown	£3.50
☐ 7497 2200 2	**Crazy Shoe Shuffle**	Gillian Cross	£3.99
☐ 7497 0592 2	**The Peacock Garden**	Anita Desai	£3.50
☐ 7497 1822 6	**Tilly Mint Tales**	Berlie Doherty	£3.50
☐ 7497 0054 8	**My Naughty Little Sister**	Dorothy Edwards	£3.50
☐ 7497 0723 2	**The Little Prince (colour ed.)**	A. Saint-Exupery	£4.50
☐ 7497 0305 9	**Bill's New Frock**	Anne Fine	£3.50
☐ 7497 1718 1	**My Grandmother's Stories**	Adèle Geras	£3.50
☐ 7497 2611 3	**A Horse for Mary Beth**	Alison Hart	£3.50
☐ 7497 1930 3	**The Jessame Stories**	Julia Jarman	£3.50
☐ 7497 0420 9	**I Don't Want To**	Bel Mooney	£3.50
☐ 7497 0048 3	**Friends and Brothers**	Dick King Smith	£3.50
☐ 7497 2596 6	**Billy Rubbish**	Alexander McCall Smith	£3.50
☐ 7497 0795 X	**Owl Who Was Afraid of the Dark**	Jill Tomlinson	£3.99

All these books are available at your bookshop or newsagent, or can be ordered direct from the address below. Just tick the titles you want and fill in the form below.

Cash Sales Department, PO Box 5, Rushden, Northants NN10 6YX.
Fax: 01933 414047 : Phone: 01933 414000.

Please send cheque, payable to 'Reed Book Services Ltd.', or postal order for purchase price quoted and allow the following for postage and packing:

£1.00 for the first book, 50p for the second; **FREE POSTAGE AND PACKING FOR THREE BOOKS OR MORE PER ORDER.**

NAME (Block letters) ....

ADDRESS...

....

☐ I enclose my remittance for...........................

☐ I wish to pay by Access/Visa Card Number ☐☐☐☐☐☐☐☐☐☐☐☐☐☐

Expiry Date ☐☐☐☐

Signature . . . .

Please quote our reference: MAND